Alice in Wonderland

s Carroll

Retold by ...rgen

Ottenheimer
PUBLISHERS, INC

One day a little girl named Alice was playing in the park near her house. Suddenly, right in front of her, a white rabbit dashed by. He was dressed up in a vest and a jacket and a top hat. As he was running by, the rabbit pulled a gold

watch from his vest pocket.

"Oh my," he cried. "I am so late. I am going to see the Queen, and she does not like anyone to be late. She is going to chop off my head. Oh dear, oh dear. Whatever shall I do?"

Now Alice had never seen a rabbit with a watch before. She was very curious, so she followed the rabbit until he disappeared into a hole in the ground. Alice looked into the hole, but she could not see anything because it was too dark. She called out to the rabbit. "Hello down there. Are you all right?" She didn't hear any answer so she bent down to have a closer look into the hole. Before she could catch herself, Alice tumbled head over heels down into the long, dark hole.

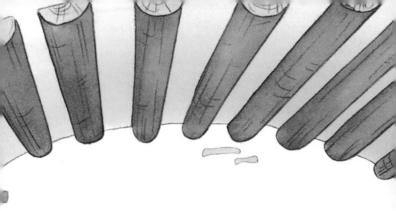

Finally, she landed in a room. Alice was very frightened because she did not know where she was. She looked around and found a door. "I will go through this door," Alice said to herself. "Then I will find my way home."

But Alice was too big to fit through the door. Then she saw a bottle on a table. "Drink me," it said. So Alice drank from the bottle. When she had finished, she became very, very small. She was small enough to fit through the door. But now she was too little to reach the key that would unlock the door.

   While she was wondering what to do, Alice saw a small cake on the table. "Eat me," it said. So Alice, who was now very hungry, ate the cake. As soon as she was finished, she began to grow very large. Soon she was too big to fit through the door.

Outside, the rabbit, who was still on his way to see the Queen, heard Alice crying. "I can't get out," she sobbed. Alice was crying so much that her tears had formed a big puddle outside. The rabbit was standing right in the middle of the puddle. He was getting very wet from Alice's tears.

The rabbit tried with all his might and finally was able to squeeze Alice through the door. "Follow me," he ordered Alice. "I'm late. We must hurry."

Alice rushed after the rabbit, but soon she lost sight of him. "Which way should I go?" she wondered aloud.

"You should go and see the Mad Hatter," said the Cheshire Cat, smiling down at her.

He appeared from nowhere! He pointed the way and then disappeared as quickly as he had appeared.

Alice soon found the house of the Mad Hatter. The Mad Hatter and his friends, the March Hare and the Dormouse, were sitting outside, having a tea party.

But before Alice could ask to join the tea party, the Mad Hatter and his friends ran off. Alice was getting very tired by now, but she followed them until they all reached the Queen's castle.

The Queen of Hearts was in her garden playing croquet—with flamingos for mallets and hedgehogs for balls!

After the game, the Queen invited Alice to have some tarts. But someone had stolen the tarts! "Off with her head!" said the Queen, pointing to Alice.

"Nonsense! You can't punish me for something I haven't done," Alice said. "Who cares for you, anyway? You're all just a bunch of cards!"

And so they were. They flew up in the air and came down upon Alice like a rain shower.

Just then, Alice heard someone whisper, "Wake up now, dear." Alice looked around and saw her mother smiling at her. And then Alice understood that the rabbit, the tea party, the croquet game, and the shower of cards were all a dream!